Lights...Camera...
Crash!

Suddenly there came a high-pitched scream from inside, then a terrible crash. John opened the door, and Sebastian scooted in ahead of him. The two of them dashed to where a crowd had gathered under the glare of bright lights.

"Quick!" a woman's voice yelled from the center of the crowd. "Get the veterinarian!"

Sebastian pushed through the tangle of legs to get to the center of the action. A big spotlight lay shattered on the floor. And right next to the light lay Chummy the Wonder Dog, and she wasn't moving.

Books by Mary Blount Christian

Sebastian (Super Sleuth) and the Purloined Sirloin
Sebastian (Super Sleuth) and the Clumsy Cowboy
Sebastian (Super Sleuth) and the Santa Claus Caper
Sebastian (Super Sleuth) and the Skewered Skier
Sebastian (Super Sleuth) and the Stars-in-His-Eyes Mystery

Published by MINSTREL Books

SEBASTIAN
(Super Sleuth)
and the
Stars-in-his-Eyes
Mystery

by
Mary Blount Christian

**Illustrated by
LISA McCUE**

A MINSTREL® BOOK

PUBLISHED BY POCKET BOOKS

New York   London   Toronto   Sydney   Tokyo

To Jennifer, who has stars in her eyes

This book is a work of fiction. Names, characters, places and incidents are either the product of the author's imagination or are used fictitiously. Any resemblance to actual events or locales or persons, living or dead, is entirely coincidental.

A Minstrel Book published by
POCKET BOOKS, a division of Simon & Schuster Inc.
1230 Avenue of the Americas, New York, NY 10020

Text copyright © 1987 by Mary Blount Christian
Illustrations copyright © 1987 by Lisa McCue
Cover art copyright © 1990 by Judith Sutton

Published by arrangement with Macmillan Publishing Company
Library of Congress Catalog Card Number: 86-21771

ISBN: 0-671-63254-X

First Minstrel Books printing January 1990

10 9 8 7 6 5 4 3 2 1

A MINSTREL BOOK and colophon are registered trademarks
of Simon & Schuster Inc.

Printed in the U.S.A.

Contents

1

In the Doghouse Again

Sebastian sniffed the couch cushion. There was a faint scent of ketchup and hamburger, possibly where he'd accidentally knocked John's burger from his hands the night before. He licked the spot. Ummm, yes. Only a bit, but still tasty. Maybe if he just scraped a little with his tiny front teeth he could —*rrrip!* A piece of fabric tore off and hung from his canine tooth as John walked in.

"Sebastian!" he yelled. "What have you done!"

What had *he* done? *He* hadn't dropped the hamburger last night. *And*, had it worked out as planned, he would have had that spot cleaned up in just another minute.

"What am I going to do with you!" John screamed again. "Any more of this, and I'm going to put you in obedience school, that's what!" John snatched the cloth from Sebastian's tooth and turned the cushion over so the tear wouldn't show. "If I weren't almost late for work, I'd— Oh, bother. Now I really *am* late. Come on!"

John wasn't the only one late for work. Detective John Quincy Jones might be the paid member of this duo, but his fuzzy buddy worked just as hard and long. Harder even, and with more success, he might add.

"Stop dawdling, Sebastian," John grumbled as he shoved him into the car. "And don't shed!"

Sebastian settled into the bucket seat, glaring at John. Stop this. Don't do that. And just because he was four-footed and hairy! Humans! Couldn't they imagine what it was like to be treated as a second-class citizen? *Imagine!* Why, John didn't even have enough imagination to go undercover, the way the old hairy hawkshaw did. (In his neverending search for criminals, this clever canine had been a bearskin rug, a gypsy dancer, and even a department store Santa Claus.)

John pulled into the police lot and parked. They went inside. "Now, don't act naughty during morning call," he warned as they slipped into the meeting room.

Sebastian rolled from his left flank to his right and yawned noisily. Precinct meetings could be so

2

boring. Officer This had just been promoted, Officer That had captured the Halloween mugger, and on and on and on. *Bor*-ing.

"And let's hear it for Detective John Quincy Jones for his part in breaking up the auto theft ring," Chief said grudgingly.

Sebastian's head popped up. John? Just John? Didn't anybody ever give credit where credit was due? Was it not he, Sebastian (Super Sleuth), who had *really* caught the thief? Was it not the old hairy hawkshaw who had donned a mechanic's coveralls to infiltrate the dangerous den of auto thievery?

Yes, the old four-on-the-floor hero Sebastian worked his paws to nubs for the City Police Department. While John and the other humans were still puzzling out the clues, he had already solved the cases.

And what thanks did he get? A pat on the head? An extra helping of mashed potatoes and gravy? No! All he ever got was, "Don't shed, Sebastian." "Stop scratching, Sebastian." "Play with your rubber bone, Sebastian."

"Stop scratching, Sebastian," John said, tapping Sebastian on the shoulder.

Curling his lip, Sebastian waited until John wasn't watching, then slipped into the hall. He was starved. He hadn't had a thing to eat in an hour.

His keen nose quivered as he suddenly caught a whiff of coffee perking in Chief's office. Where there was coffee, there might be doughnuts. Doughnuts just oozing with jelly or soft pudding. Or glistening with sugar glaze. He licked the drool from his whiskers and padded through Chief's door.

Good. Chief was still droning away at the meeting. Now, where would he have hidden the goodies? Chief *always* hid the goodies because he was always on a diet, and he didn't want others to know that he sneaked food.

Sebastian looked behind the potted plant. He looked on top of the desk, under a stack of papers, scattering them in all directions. He looked in the bookcase, knocking volumes of police procedure and law theory to the floor.

No, the smell was definitely stronger near the filing cabinet. Sebastian sniffed. Yes, in the filing cabinet. He pawed at the closed drawer, whimpering.

"Here, now," Chief yelled as he stormed into the room. "Get away from there, you walking garbage disposal!"

John rushed in behind him. "But, Chief!" he exclaimed. "He's after something. It could be a bomb. You know how sensitive his nose is."

"No," Chief said, flustered. "That stupid dog is always—"

"Stand back, Chief!" John said. "We wouldn't want *you* to get hurt. I'll check it out. Don't get near it!"

"But—"

John eased the cabinet door open ever so gently and cautiously peered inside. His shoulders heaved with a sigh. "Oh, it's only doughnuts." He looked up at Chief apologetically. "I—I'm sorry about the scratches on your cabinet." He narrowed his eyes at Sebastian. "And the jumble of papers and books. His manners have been deplorable lately!"

Sebastian rumbled under his breath. John was working himself into a snit over nothing. What were a few scattered papers and books? Surely John wouldn't put him through obedience training for that!

Chief sucked in his bulging stomach. "Those doughnuts aren't mine! Somebody must have put them in there. Some kind of a joke."

"Oh, then I'll just take them out of here, Chief. We wouldn't want to tempt you, now, would we?" John said, grinning.

"Set those down!" Chief demanded. "I need to talk to you about a new case."

John put the doughnuts on Chief's desk and sat in the chair opposite him.

Sebastian edged closer to the doughnuts, drool

gathering at the corners of his mouth. He swallowed hard and leaned forward as close as he could.

Chief slid the doughnuts farther from the edge of the desk and opened a file, removing a photograph. Sebastian recognized the subject right away. It was that overweight, overrated movie star, Chummy the Wonder Dog. Would their paths cross again? Was Chummy in trouble once more?

2
Boning Up

Sebastian listened intently as Chief described the case.

"Chummy the Wonder Dog is starring in a new made-for-television movie," Chief began. "There's been some trouble on the set—accidents that have resulted in injuries and damaged equipment. Chummy's owners are worried about her safety. They suspect foul play." Chief made a face. "Don't ask me why, but they've specifically asked for you and that mangy dog of yours."

Sebastian crept a little closer to the doughnuts. They had asked for the old cagey canine, had they? *Some* people recognized genius when they saw it. He had saved their stupid dog from a kidnap plot before, and they rightfully appreciated his efforts. Now they needed his help again. He panted smugly.

"Chief, I haven't read about a movie being made here," John said.

"It's *not* being made here, Jones. Chummy's in Hollywood. Her owners are sending their private Lear jet to pick you two up. It's already on its way. You've got two hours to pack a few things and get to the airport," Chief said, handing John a file marked CHUMMY.

Sebastian felt dizzy with joy. It was not because he would be seeing Chummy again. Even seeing her movies on television annoyed him. But Hollywood! Private jet! And *he* had been *requested*! Recognized at last!

John accepted the file, open-mouthed. "Airport," he finally muttered. "Two hours."

"They want this to be strictly an undercover job, Detective Jones," Chief said. "Only Chummy's owners know your real identity. The others on the set will think you are a dog trainer brought in by the owners. That mutt will be your perfect cover. Heaven help us all, he'll actually be in the movie."

Sebastian sucked in one of the jelly doughnuts and swallowed. He wagged the stub of his tail excitedly. He did a quick roll on the rug, then leaped into the air, yipping. He was going to be a movie star! Sebastian executed a canine cartwheel. Then

9

he snapped up one more doughnut—chocolate cream.

"Get that fleabag out of my office before he breaks something and eats all of my—er, somebody's—doughnuts," Chief growled.

John jumped up and shoved the CHUMMY file under his arm. "Thanks, Chief!"

Chief reached to retrieve some of his papers, muttering, "Don't thank *me*, Jones. I assure you, you and that hairy garbage can wouldn't be my first choice."

John turned and walked briskly from the room, singing "California, Here I Come." Sebastian fell into a trot alongside John. He had left Chief the last doughnut. It had a lemon filling—not his personal favorite, anyway.

All the way to the car, Sebastian concentrated on holding his chin parallel to the floor and placing each foot in a proper straight line. That was the stride of the stars!

At home John threw a few things into a suitcase and darted back to the car. It was all Sebastian could do to keep up with him.

When John and Sebastian reached the airport, the jet, a gleaming white, stood ready for them. Unfortunately, the plane bore a likeness of Chummy, and her name was on its nose. Sebastian was willing to overlook that, however, since inside was a canine palace at his disposal.

The cabin had a well-stocked refrigerator filled with doggie delights, and not a single box of those awful Chummy Yummies, the dry dog food Chummy advertised. Ha! He didn't think she *really* ate them. *Crummy* Yummies, he called them. Her owners had given him a year's supply after he'd solved her case. He'd scattered them all over the backyard. Since that stuff was for the birds, he figured it ought to go to them.

Sebastian noted that there was a four-poster, cedar-filled bed just his size on board. It was an exact replica of the one Chummy had in her mobile dressing room, spoiled creature. And there was a shower that gently massaged all the itchy spots with soothing streams of warm water.

This time, when John insisted on bathing him, Sebastian didn't fuss. And when Sebastian mischievously shook the water all over him, John didn't even lose his temper and threaten him with obedience school.

Using the hair dryer, John gently fluffed and dried his fur. Then they settled into the plush seats for the remainder of the trip. This was the life!

All in all, it was a fantasy trip. And by the time they landed at LAX—as Californians call Los

Angeles International Airport—Sebastian was rested and ready for a mystery, and for stardom.

Although the flight took three hours, the detective duo arrived only an hour later than they'd left. That was because California time was two hours earlier than their state's.

A limousine waited at the airport for John and Sebastian. Its windows were tinted so dark that no one could see inside. A uniformed chauffeur tipped his hat and opened the door for them, and they were whisked down the freeway and through the busy streets to the studio.

"Don't drool on the upholstery," John whispered to Sebastian.

Sebastian looked at him narrowly. Didn't John realize that he was griping at the most important part of this team. Without the hairy hawkshaw, he'd have no cover to go under!

Sebastian sat proudly erect on the rear seat as the limo was waved through the security booth at the studio gate. The chauffeur turned around and spoke to John. "They're shooting in that big, barnlike building, Studio 28. I'll let you out there. But wait outside if the red light is flashing, sir."

They drove past 1929 and 1930 Fords and Chevrolets, polished to a sparkle, and people dressed in Roaring Twenties costumes. Then they passed others in Indian costumes and some in Western outfits with horses.

There must be many movies being made at the same time, Sebastian figured. He twitched excitedly as he and John got out and the big limo rolled away.

On the door to Studio 28, there was a red sign that said WARNING. WHEN LIGHT IS FLASHING, CAMERAS ARE ROLLING. DO NOT ENTER. The light was flashing. John leaned against the building, waiting. Sebastian sat down and watched the light.

Suddenly there came a high-pitched scream from inside, then a terrible crash. John opened the door, and Sebastian scooted in ahead of him. The two of them dashed to where a crowd had gathered under the glare of bright lights.

"Quick!" a woman's voice yelled from the center of the crowd. "Get the veterinarian!"

Sebastian pushed through the tangle of legs to get to the center of the action. A big spotlight lay shattered on the floor. And right next to the light lay Chummy the Wonder Dog, and she wasn't moving.

3
A Hero's Welcome

"She's only fainted," the veterinarian said after examining Chummy the Wonder Dog. He held a bottle of something under her nose.

Chummy's nose twitched. Then her eyelids fluttered open, and she whimpered pitifully. The crash probably had just scared her. She rolled to a sitting position, and the crowd of people sighed almost simultaneously.

Sebastian sniffed. He wondered if she'd really fainted, or if she had been faking it to get attention. After all, she hadn't changed since the last time he'd seen her, during the Crummy Yummies Caper. She was the same tinted, powdered phony. Was that her *real* fur? he wondered. Or was she wearing one of those fake fur coats he'd seen in her dressing room when he'd rescued her at the dog show?

Chummy blinked and looked around groggily. She spotted Sebastian and yipped with joy. Struggling heavily to her feet, she licked the side of his fuzzy face.

Sebastian groaned, redfaced. He was sure everyone could see the blush right through his fur. Of course Chummy adored the old sleuth. He'd saved her singlehandedly, hadn't he? But he certainly didn't want this kind of affection. It was humiliating, especially since some of the humans standing around were giggling and saying how cute it was.

He nodded politely to Chummy, then moved away from her as quickly as he could. He had work to do. The vet led Chummy back to her dressing room to rest, and the others soon ignored him, thank goodness!

Sebastian stared up at the ceiling thirty feet above, where the big light had hung before it fell. Chief had said there were accidents on the set. Was this an accident, too? Or had someone *made* the light fall?

"Take a fifteen-minute break!" a woman in gray slacks and a white blouse shouted. Her small frame slumped into a folding canvas chair that said DIRECTOR on the back. She pinched her eyes shut with her fingers. "Carlton is in his office gloating, I just know it!" she muttered. "He never wanted me to direct this picture."

Sebastian recalled seeing the name Carlton at the main gate. A sign said that he was president of

Marvelous Film Studios. Could Carlton be willing to sabotage one of his own films to get rid of the director? If so, the cagey canine would find out!

Most of the crowd shuffled noisily over to a table where coffee and sandwiches had been set out. Several men with brooms and dustpans began cleaning up the shattered glass and tangle of metal that had landed right in the middle of the set.

Sebastian skulked to the table, edging between people's legs. He gulped down a couple of tuna fish sandwiches—*burp*—then slipped away into the shadows.

Among the lights and wires in the ceiling high above them, he spotted a catwalk. (How he hated that word.) He wanted to get a better look at where the light had been.

A tiny, cagelike elevator against the west wall would take him to the catwalk. Sebastian got in and nosed the button that said UP. He gritted his teeth as the elevator jerked and began to rise. If only he could overcome his fear of heights....

The elevator shuddered to a halt at the top. Cautiously Sebastian made his way out, testing with each paw before moving forward on the narrow metal grating. No wonder they called this a *cat*walk. Only cats were lightweight—and stupid—enough to take this trip easily four stories up.

The catwalk trembled slightly. He decided to

belly-crawl the rest of the way. It was hard to see how this thing could take the weight of a grown-up human, unless the human was small—like the woman in gray slacks, who must be the director.

He finally made it to the spot where the light had been. Even in the dim light he could see fresh scratches on the metal frame and the supporting cables. It looked as if the bolts had been deliberately removed. And the cables were not torn the way they would have been if they had worn out. Their ends were even and crisp. They had been cut nearly in two. Sebastian figured that the weight of the heavy light must have finished the job—but not before the culprit had returned safely to the floor.

This was no accident. Somebody was trying to kill Chummy the Wonder Dog. Or at the very least make her too scared to finish the film.

Sebastian made his way back to the elevator and down to the main floor, where he joined the others in another round of sandwiches. This time he sneaked peanut butter and jelly when no one was looking.

As he tried to unstick the peanut butter from the roof of his mouth, he studied the crowd of people. Who among them was the culprit? Was it that grumpy-faced man with the can of film under his arm, or maybe that woman scribbling in the margin

of a script? Or was the criminal not there at all but somewhere else, dreaming up more devilish things to do? The old hairy hawkshaw liked a challenge, but he could do with fewer suspects. After all, he didn't want to spend *all* his time detecting. He had *acting* to do.

Sebastian spotted John talking to a man with a purple Mohawk haircut and mismatched earrings. He snatched another sandwich, then moved quietly to the side to get a different perspective of the huge, barnlike structure.

It was a whole new world inside this building. Backdrops—scenes of mountains and water—and furniture were all jammed together. It meant a million places to hide, and a million ways to hurt someone and still make it seem like an accident. Why, there was even a big water tank made to look like a small lagoon. Someone could easily "fall" into it.

The huge room remained mostly dark, except in the area where the film was being shot. Bright lights shone there on what looked almost like a real home. The rooms had only three walls, though, and no ceilings.

Sebastian edged his way over by John as the woman in gray slacks and a white blouse rushed up to his human. "I'm Jessica Mitchner, the director of this mixed blessing. You're John Q. Jones? Chummy's owners said they'd taken care of getting your dog. Thank goodness you're both here."

Sebastian panted smugly. They were waiting for him.

"Chummy is all right now and ready to resume shooting," Ms. Mitchner said. "We've got a scene coming up where we need your dog. Time is money. Let's go, go, go!"

But what about his lines? His motivation? What did the scene involve? Wasn't he going to get any direction?

"Break's over!" she shouted. "Positions, everybody!"

John followed the woman and tapped her on the shoulder. "Er, pardon me, but does Sebastian look all right?" John asked. "I had him groomed, but—"

"Nobody's going to care, believe me." She turned to someone else, shouting an order. "Get that Chummy suit on him, and hurry."

Now wait a minute. Chummy suit? What was going on here? He would play a canine Hamlet or even King Lear, but hide this handsome body and face in a *St. Bernard* disguise? Never!

A man in a T-shirt that said HUG ME, I'M WONDERFUL came up and strapped a mahogany-colored fur coat onto Sebastian. Another man began

21

smearing dark, gooey makeup on Sebastian's face and ears. *Phew!*

"He doesn't look like a St. Bernard," John said, "not even with all that makeup."

The man in the T-shirt glanced at John. "Nobody's going to notice. Trust me. We do this with stunt people all the time when there's dang—"

"Quiet on the set!" someone shouted.

"Okay, Rod," Jessica Mitchner said. "Get Chummy to grab Amanda's dress collar and drag her to the window. She should pause at the window, then jump, okay?"

"Right," the man called Rod said, "no problem."

Sebastian figured Rod was Chummy's new manager. The super sleuth and his partner had had the old one arrested and put away for kidnapping and extortion.

Rod led Chummy from her dressing room, and Amanda, the child actress, got on the floor and pretended to be unconscious.

"Gas jets on!" someone shouted.

Suddenly the scene looked as if it were in flames.

"Lights! Cameras! Action!" Ms. Mitchner shouted.

Rod hand-signaled, and Chummy began dragging the little girl to the window. Actually, the little girl was on some sort of board with wheels, so Chummy could pull her without strain. That wouldn't show on film. What a cheat! He'd known all along what a fake this Hollywood stuff was!

Chummy got to the window, leaping up onto the sill to pause dramatically before jumping. Big deal. It was only six inches to the floor.

"Cut!" Jessica Mitchner yelled. "Bring in the substitute."

"It's your turn," a young woman in a bright pink dress told John. "My name's Rachel, and I'm Jessica's assistant, by the way. Come with me, and I'll get you up there."

Up where? What did she mean? What was going on?

Rachel led John and Sebastian to another part of the big studio. It looked like the outside of a two-story house. In front of it, some men were pumping up a big, balloonlike mattress on the floor.

Rachel motioned for them to follow her behind the house. It was only a wall. Behind it were a scaffold, steps, and a platform.

Sebastian hesitated at the foot of the steps. Going up in the elevator had been bad enough. But climb the rickety steps up to that little platform? No way.

John tugged on the slip-chain collar, and Sebastian followed reluctantly.

On the platform was a life-sized rag doll dressed just like the little girl. Wait a minute! A doll that

24

looked like the girl, Sebastian dressed to look like Chummy, and a second-story window. It was all starting to make sense. Nonsense, rather.

"Now, if I were you," Rachel said, "I'd give that inflated mattress a last-minute check, then not leave it until the stunt was over."

"What do you mean?" John asked. "Is there some problem with the stunt?"

Yeah, what did she mean?

"Jessica doesn't want us talking about all this, but it's why your dog has this job. Somebody forgot to close off the release valve and let most of the air out of the mattress yesterday. The poor stunt dog sprained all four ankles in this scene. And they didn't even get the scene on film. Apparently, somebody forgot to load the camera with film, although I can't imagine such a thing."

John frowned. "Sounds like a lot of forgetting on this set," he said.

Rachel shrugged. "Sam swears he closed the valve himself. And Jerry said he put the film in the camera. He even asked for a lie detector test to prove it. But what's the use? The damage was done."

Sebastian wrapped his paws around John's leg and whimpered. How could John put his faithful companion and super-duper detective partner in danger!

4
What Goes Up...

John peered through the window. He turned to Rachel. "Are you sure this is perfectly safe? Sebastian is my chum, my little buddy. I won't put him in any danger, no sir."

That was more like it. Chum, little buddy, and he shouldn't forget fantastic furry sleuth. A rare animal.

Rachel smiled at John and patted Sebastian on the head. "We have a member of the Humane Society present on the set at all times. He'd never let us endanger an animal. And Jessica loves animals, too. She wouldn't ask your dog to do anything she wouldn't do herself."

Then let her do it! The cagey canine would gladly step aside. They did say no one would notice or care.

John nodded, then bent to whisper in Sebastian's ear. "Now, Sebastian, old fellow, I'll just go downstairs, and when I whistle, you come to me."

Sebastian wasn't arguing about going downstairs. But jump? Was John kidding?

Rachel scratched Sebastian's ear. "I'll just strap this dolly to his costume here," she said. "It'll look as if he's holding it. Then all he has to do is jump!"

All? Just jump? That was *all*?

John gave Sebastian one last pat on the head, then followed Rachel down the steps. "Stay," he commanded.

Sebastian slumped to the platform, sulking. How did he ever get into a mess like this? He should be a star, not a stunt dog. He'd just sit out the day right here, and they'd be sorry.

What was taking so long down there, anyway? He rose to peek out the fake window. He could see that the big, balloonlike mattress was all plumped up now. John was walking around it, inspecting it for leaks that might let the air out too fast, should somebody jump on it. He was wasting his time. *This* somebody was not going to jump! They were using a fake child. Why couldn't they use a fake Chummy, too? A rag Chummy?

Someone had pointed the cameras toward the

window just past the heads of a man, a woman, and a little boy who were standing at the bottom of the fake house.

"All right," Ms. Mitchner shouted above the noise of the people milling around. "Lilly, Sanders, and little Tommy, let's get this in one take, okay? Places, everyone. John, are you and Sebastian ready?"

"Ready," John said. He was grinning from ear to ear. Of course John had something to grin about: *He* wasn't going to jump. Well, neither was the super sleuth, thank you.

"Effects, lights, cameras, action!" Ms. Mitchner shouted.

Effects? What effects? Suddenly from behind Sebastian there came a hissing sound. He sniffed. Smoke! *Hack, hack. Ah-hooey!*

"My child!" Lilly screamed. "My child is in there!" She stretched her arms toward the window, then fainted.

Sanders, who was leaning on crutches, said, "I'll never make it in there! What'll we do? Oh, help us, somebody, help!"

This movie needed help. It stank even more than the smoke. *Hack, hack. Ah-hooey!*

Little Tommy stepped forward. "Don't worry, sir! My brave dog will save your little girl. Get her,

Chummy! Fetch the little girl! Jump into this basket of laundry!"

Phooey! If Chummy was going to get the credit, let Chummy jump! *Hack, hack.*

John whistled.

John could forget it. Sebastian was going to find the steps and go down the sensible way. *Hack.* If he could just find his way through this smoke. He couldn't tell if he was heading to or from the window.

Suddenly a dark figure reached out and wrapped its fingers tightly around him. Sebastian struggled, trying to get away. He jerked hard, and the fingers lost their grip.

Sebastian felt himself tumbling through the window. Flailing his paws frantically, he landed with a *whoosh* on the billowy air mattress and floated up and down as it settled under his weight.

"Good fellow!" John shouted, grabbing for him.

Sebastian eyed the crowd narrowly. Somebody had grabbed him. But who? Was it somebody Jessica Mitchner had sent up to make sure he jumped? Or was it the same person who'd tried to hurt the stunt dog before him and Chummy?

No face looked more guilty than any other. Everyone just seemed relieved that the scene was over.

Sebastian rumbled low in his throat. This job was not turning out at all as he'd expected. Now he knew that not everything in Hollywood was fake—at least not the stunts!

Sebastian's foot thumped rhythmically as John stroked behind his furry ears. He watched the crew hurriedly deflating the air mattress.

When they had removed the mattress from the set, they rolled out a carpet of fake grass and even a tree and flower garden. They brought out a big basket of unfolded laundry. Chummy and the little girl got on top of the laundry, and Ms. Mitchner directed the crew to take their picture. When the film had been edited, it probably would look as if Chummy had jumped through the window and landed with the girl in the laundry.

"Break for lunch," Jessica Mitchner said afterward. She strode away with the script tucked under her arm.

Rachel came up. She helped John remove Sebastian's Chummy suit. They wiped the makeup from his face and ears. That was better.

"Follow the crowd to the commissary," she said. "They've set up box lunches there. You can leave your dog in the kennel just outside, where they have food and water for him."

John led Sebastian to the small fenced area and

shut him in. "I'll be along in a few minutes," John told Rachel. "I'll find it on my own, thanks."

He probably was going to hang back, then go in and check the place where the fallen light had hung. Good! That would save Sebastian the trouble of trying to tell John about it.

Sebastian glanced around the kennel. The pits! Chummy would be lolling around in her own picture-perfect dressing room, John was going with the others to the commissary, and he, Sebastian (Super Sleuth), was stuck here in a three-by-five concrete kennel with a bowl of dry dog food.

Was this any way to solve a mystery?

5

Pirating Clues

Sebastian rose on his hind legs and studied the gate closure. No problem. It was a simple lift latch. He nosed it up and leaned against the gate. It swung open.

Sebastian dashed out and headed for the commissary. Let John look for clues in the studio. The cagey canine would find tastier places to look.

He skidded to a quick stop. He had better find a disguise. He didn't want John to spot him away from the kennel and start talking about obedience school again. And as long as these people thought of him as an ordinary stunt dog, they probably would throw him out the minute he turned up in the lunch line. But in a masterful disguise he could ramble unnoticed among them, perhaps pick up clues—and a decent lunch.

He looked around. There was the wardrobe building. Sebastian slipped through the open door and found row upon row of costumes on racks. But what to take? Southern belle? Astronaut? Cowboy? Clown? There! A pirate's outfit would be perfect.

Quickly Sebastian slipped his back legs into the striped pantaloons and black boots. He wiggled into the eye patch and head scarf with its attached earring. He whirled before the mirror. Would this be sufficient, or did he need a mustache?

Confident that he looked not only undoggie but also appropriately dashing, Sebastian bounded toward the commissary. There he got into line and was handed a box. It smelled like bologna and apples. No doubt Chummy was having a steak.

Settling into the first empty chair he found, Sebastian shook the box vigorously. The lid flew up. He nipped at the wrapping around the sandwich and spat it out.

A man and a woman sat down at the table. He recognized them from the Chummy set.

"I didn't know there was a pirate film on the lot right now," the man said.

Ummm. Sebastian hadn't thought about that.

"Oh, I bet you're in the dream sequence of the twenties film, aren't you?" the woman guessed.

Ummm. Sebastian breathed a sigh of relief.

"I'll bet pirates ate in just as unmannerly a way as you're eating!" the man said. "You always stay in character, even on lunch breaks?"

Ummm, ummm, Sebastian whined. What did the guy mean, unmannerly? How would he like to have paws? He swallowed half the sandwich.

"It's probably best to stay in character during breaks," the woman said. "It saves you the trouble of working yourself back into it later. Of course, our star is always in character. Get it? Chummy is always a dog!" She sniggered.

Sebastian opened his mouth in a panting grin. *Huh, huh.* Chummy didn't have his expertise. He swallowed the other half of his sandwich.

The man and woman turned to their own conversation, leaving him to his lunch—and to eavesdropping. Part of being a good detective was being a good listener.

"I'll be glad when they finish this film, won't you?" the man asked. "It gives me the creeps, the way weird things keep happening."

The woman nodded. "If you ask me, this movie's jinxed. First the set catches fire and has to be rebuilt. Then the camera falls off the boom and smashes and we have to wait for a replacement. Then the water tank ruptures and floods the set. The mattress is deflated, injuring the stunt dog. And now, today, that light nearly hits Chummy. I'll tell you, I don't feel safe."

"Just don't stand anywhere near the stars, that's

all," the man said. "Anyway, you may not have to worry much longer. I hear rumors that Leroy Carlton may shut it down. As a part-time accountant—when I'm not acting, of course—I can tell you we'll probably be over budget by the end of today. Poor Horace. He's worked so hard to raise the money for this film, too. I sure wouldn't want to be a producer and have to tell all those investors that their money is down the drain."

Sebastian leaned over his lunch box, sniffing. He located a blueberry muffin and swallowed it in one slurp.

He reviewed the incidents the woman had named. The set was burned, then flooded, and the camera equipment was smashed. But the harm was only to things, not people. Then the stunt dog was injured, though, and Chummy was nearly crushed beneath a big light. He, Sebastian, had been shoved from the window by unseen hands. Unless, of course, the mysterious figure had been trying to hold him back. Now that he thought about it, it did seem that he had been more pulled than pushed. And that would make sense if someone was trying to keep the scene from being a success.

The incidents were getting more dangerous. It convinced Sebastian that someone wanted to stop the production, and when damage to the set didn't do it, that someone got more desperate. But why shut down the film? And who would want to do that?

Sebastian pawed through his lunch box, looking for more goodies. These boxes didn't have enough food in them.

Chummy's owners had asked Sebastian and John in on the case, so that let them out. No criminal in his right mind would want to go up against the daring duo.

There was this Carlton fellow, who was president of the studios and who didn't want Jessica Mitchner to direct the movie—or so she had said. Maybe he was making sure she didn't succeed. But wouldn't his studios lose a lot of money this way?

And there was Jessica Mitchner, the director, but she needed this success. Of course, maybe she knew how bad the script was. Sebastian had heard this film was her first. Maybe she wanted to kill it and make her directing debut with a better one.

Sebastian found an apple in the box—not his favorite snack, but it would have to do. He nodded good-bye to the man and woman, who got up, leaving their boxes on the table.

He checked them out—empty. How could humans make such pigs of themselves? Really!

Sebastian spotted Jessica Mitchner leaving the

37

commissary. She looked really angry. He decided to follow her.

She went straight to the executive building and, without even knocking, pushed through a door marked LEROY T. CARLTON, PRESIDENT, MARVELOUS FILM STUDIOS. Sebastian peeked in and saw that there was no one in the outer office, so he crept close and put his ear to the door, listening intently.

"What does this note I found in my postbox mean?" Jessica Mitchner demanded. She sounded furious.

A man's voice, whiny and high-pitched, answered. "Exactly what it says. You must shut down the film. Marvelous Film Studios is no longer willing to back you."

"Back me!" Jessica said. "When have you backed me? None of the money is coming from you. You have nothing to lose if it fails, and everything to gain if it succeeds. And what Chummy film has ever failed, regardless of poor scripts? Poor Horace has raised all our money, and we pay you a goodly amount of it for studio and prop rental. You just *want* to see me fail! That's what, you—you male chauvinist!"

A long sigh escaped through the keyhole. Then Jessica Mitchner spoke again. "I'll talk to Horace about getting more financial backing—"

"It's too late. Your time is up. We have another

film scheduled for that studio, a real blockbuster with that French actress, what's-her-name," the voice that must be Carlton's said. "We want you out."

"What's-her-name! That's just my point, Carlton! You don't even know her name. You don't even care! All you care about is the almighty dollars you'll make!" Jessica shrieked. More calmly, she said, "We're behind schedule because of all the incidents. If your security were better—"

"Our security takes care of the main gate and patrols outside the buildings—and here, of course. You are supposed to be taking care of security inside the studio," Carlton said. "That was our agreement." He paused. "You're not going to cry, are you?"

"No, I am not going to cry. I am going to fight!" Jessica said. "Horace hired our own security man. We just need a little time to—"

"It doesn't change anything, Jessica. Your time is up in the studio."

Her voice rose. "Just about everything left to shoot has to be done outdoors, anyway. We'll get out, Carlton. But you'll be sorry!"

The door swung open with a jerk, nearly throwing Sebastian to the floor. He regained his balance quickly, then dashed from the building before Jessica could get a good look at him.

Sebastian realized that lunch break would be over, and he'd better be where he was supposed to be when John came looking for him. He rushed back to the wardrobe building and shook free of the costume, then hurried to the kennel. He slipped inside the fence and waited for John.

"Gee," John said, patting him on the head. "You haven't touched your food. You'll waste away to nothing if you don't eat, old fellow."

Sebastian ducked his head and slunk past John. That would make his human feel properly guilty for locking his fuzzy buddy in a kennel!

When they got into the studio, Sebastian saw Jessica Mitchner in an animated conversation with some shrunken little guy behind thick glasses, wearing a stained tie and rumpled gray suit. "Horace, I thought you were different!" she yelled. "But now you're saying we ought to shut down, too?"

"I'm the producer, the money man," Horace said, "and I'm telling you we have just enough to pay off the crew and get out with our own salaries if we stop now."

"I'll give up my salary for now," Jessica said. "The executives could delay our salaries until the profits start to come in. What about you, Horace?"

"If it would help, Jessica," Horace said, "you know I would, even though I have to make payments on my secondhand car and my modest house and the retirement home for my dear mother. But it wouldn't help. Our salaries wouldn't run the studio for two hours."

"Then find more angels!" she stormed.

"We can't go out and get more angels," Horace said. He patted a ledger he held tightly in his arms. "You set up the company yourself, Jessica. We promised them each one quarter of the investors' share of the profits for their money. There are only four quarters in a hundred percent, you know."

"They'll get their investment back, and then some," Jessica said. "But that's only if the film gets to the public. If it doesn't, they'll lose their money. Can't you explain that to them? Maybe they'd be willing to pay a little more and get a little less than they expected. We're so close to finishing."

"I'll try, Jessica," Horace said. "But I won't guarantee results. I want to go on record as saying we should shut down before something really terrible happens."

Jessica squared her chin defiantly. "Then let me talk to the angels. I'm afraid with your attitude you won't be persuasive in asking for more money." She snatched the book Horace was carrying. "I'll call them myself." She thumbed through the book.

Horace pulled the ledger from Jessica's grasp.

"I'm hurt to the core that you don't trust me to do my best, Jessica."

"Wha— Why, you don't have names in there! Just numbers one through four!" Jessica said.

Horace fingered his glasses nervously. "That's so they can remain just the way they wanted—anonymous. I can't tell you the names of the investors. If you knew their names, then soon another person would know, then another and another, and finally the press would know, and they would no longer be anonymous. I promised that no one else would know their names. I'll talk to them."

"It isn't fair!" Jessica stormed. "You shouldn't be so secretive with me, Horace!" But she was speaking to his back. He was already hurrying away with his book.

Sebastian sat down and scratched his ear, puzzling out what he'd heard. He remembered hearing the term *angels* before. It was what show business people called those who gave them money to make a film. If the film was successful and made money, the angels got their investment back, and they got a percentage of the profits, too.

But if the film was not successful, they didn't get their money back at all. And there was nothing less successful than a film that was never finished!

6
Here an Angel, There an Angel

Jessica Mitchner called for silence on the set. The crew gathered close, listening. "We're going to shoot just one more scene in this studio today," she said. "Then, tomorrow, we'll shoot on location at Toppen's Lake. That'll be the big scene where Chummy's reunited with her master. Just a couple more days' shooting there, and we'll be finished. All that'll remain will be the editing. Your job will be over," she said.

Nobody looked unhappy about that!

Jessica asked Rod to bring Chummy from her dressing room. They were going to shoot the laundry basket scene again. She muttered something about a bad camera angle on the Wonder Dog.

Had they used a more superior-looking dog—say, himself—they wouldn't have had such worries.

44

Unlike Chummy, he looked good from the front, side, *and* back.

Sebastian could see John edging through the crowd, starting up conversations with crew members. Maybe they could compare notes later. As for now, he, Sebastian (Super Sleuth), would follow that Horace fellow. He seemed to do a lot of important work for the film company—getting the financial backing, arranging for sets and locations, even hiring the security (except for the old hairy hawkshaw and his human).

Sebastian slipped cautiously through the legs of the crowd and out the door. There was Horace, just about to enter a small brick building across the parking lot from the studio and next to the executive building.

Sebastian made a detour into the wardrobe building. If disguises were so conveniently located on all his cases, how easy his job would be. He knew what he wanted. He just had to spot it. There, hanging on the third rack.

He slipped into the starched black dress and stiff white apron and dust cap. He snatched the duster between his teeth and trotted toward the building he'd seen Horace enter, confident that he looked every bit the part of a maid.

Inside, he could hear Horace talking. Sebastian

followed the sound and peered into the room. Horace was sitting at a desk, and he was on the phone. He didn't look so rumpled and shy now.

"Angel," he said, "Hawaii sounds fantastic, but I was thinking more about Brazil or one of those little islands in the Caribbean."

Sebastian trotted in and began dusting the desk. That was odd. He knew that these investors were called angels, but to their faces?

"Gotta go, sweetheart," Horace said. "I've got some clearing out to do here. Go on and pack. And make the reservations. It's in the bag, as far as I'm concerned."

Horace turned and frowned toward Sebastian. "You gotta do that right now, dear?"

Sebastian ducked his head and dusted frantically. *Ummm, ummm,* he whined.

That hadn't been one of the investors on the phone with Horace. It had been some woman he called "Angel," and Horace wanted her to pack their bags. He certainly hadn't had time to call the angels, as he'd promised. It hadn't taken Sebastian long to locate a disguise.

He, Sebastian (Super Sleuth), understood now. Horace wanted Jessica Mitchner to fail. He wanted the movie not to be finished. But why? And was he somehow helping it to fail? Had *he* caused all

those accidents? He certainly was small enough to creep along the catwalk without causing it to tremble too much and give him away.

Sebastian had noticed the ledger that Horace had shown Jessica on top of the desk. Now, from the corner of his eye, he saw Horace unlock a desk drawer and pull out an identical ledger. It even had the name of the film, CHUMMY SAVES THE DAY, on the front of it. Why would Horace have two sets of books that were exactly alike? Or were they alike?

Sebastian worked his duster closer. He leaned forward and peered at the pages. He counted names —one, two, three, four . . . eight. Eight names. Wait a minute. Hadn't Horace said there were four investors, or angels? They would expect to get their original investment back. And they would each expect twenty-five percent of the investors' share of the profits. Eight people would only be able to get half of that. For a money man, Horace was not a very good mathematician. No wonder the company was in trouble.

A knock on the door made Sebastian and Horace jump. Horace jammed the second book back into the drawer and locked it. He slipped the key into the pocket of his jacket. "Yeah?" he said.

A short, thin man in an ill-fitting uniform came in. "I don't want this job anymore. People blame me for all the accidents. I'm no security man. I told you when I took this job that I'm a comedian. I got a job on the East Coast for two weeks."

Horace leaned forward. "But you promised you'd stick with the job until I told you it was over."

"But I didn't know so many bad things would happen. I don't know anything about checking out security. Oh, I can see that everybody has the right identification badge. And I can stop somebody from smoking around the scenery. But I don't know how to look for sabotage and stuff like that."

Horace shrugged. He reached for a stack of pink papers and signed one, handing it to the man. "Everybody will be getting dismissal slips soon enough. Here, take this to the front office and get your pay. And good luck with your new act."

"Thanks, Mr. Roland, and I hope the picture comes out okay. I'm sorry I wasn't very good at security."

Horace waved him away, and the man left.

Curious. Why wouldn't Horace hire a real security man? Didn't he know that this comedian wouldn't know what to look for or how to avoid trouble? Or was it that he didn't want someone who knew?

Horace glared at Sebastian. "Aren't you through yet, dear? You certainly are a slow one."

49

Sebastian hovered over the bookcase, dusting furiously.

Horace removed his jacket and hung it on the back of his chair. He walked to the water cooler and poured himself a drink. While his back was turned, Sebastian scooted over and hastily poked his nose into the jacket pocket to retrieve the key. Ooops! He snagged a patch of the pocket, too.

Quickly he dropped the patch and the key into his uniform pocket and hurried from the room. He could go back later and check the book. He only hoped that Horace wouldn't notice the torn pocket.

Sebastian trotted toward the wardrobe building to return the maid's uniform. He mulled over all he had found out. What did he know?

He knew that Horace had promised Jessica he would ask the angels for more backing, but he had not called them. And he knew that Horace had a ledger in a locked drawer listing eight angels. He had told Jessica that there were four—and that he could not reveal their names because they wanted to remain anonymous.

Sebastian shut his eyes and tried to remember. After each name was a dollar sign and lots of zeros —enough to make two million dollars by each name. Horace had said that the angels were to get twenty-five percent of the investors' profits. But

eight times twenty-five percent made two hundred percent.

Hold it! That was it! Horace had too many angels. If the movie was a success, each angel would expect twenty-five percent of the profits—one hundred percent more than there would be. But if the movie was never completed, no one would know the difference. Horace would be pocketing eight million dollars.

No wonder he wanted to go to Brazil. He figured nobody could touch him there. He—and someone he called "Angel"—would be free to live with his ill-gotten gains. The old hairy hawkshaw had done it again! Now, how was he going to let his human know?

7
Sebastian Saves the Day

Sebastian returned the costume. Clutching the key and the patch of pocket in his mouth, he hurried back to John, who was sitting in the director's chair, writing in his notebook. A quick peek convinced Sebastian that John also had figured out that the light had been sabotage.

He dropped the key and pocket patch on top of John's notebook.

John's eyes widened. "Oh, no! Sebastian! What have you done? You've bitten somebody! And taken his key? Oh, now we're in trouble! That does it, Sebastian. That really does it. It's the obedience school for you! Jessica? Oh, Jessica!" he called.

She walked over with her hands on her hips. "Yes?"

"I think there's been some trouble," he said. "Do you recognize this material?"

She studied the fabric. "That's from Horace's

jacket," she said. "I just saw him in it."

"I'm afraid my dog may have injured him. And he took this," John said, handing her the key. "I'm so sorry. I don't know what's come over him lately."

Jessica Mitchner sighed. "Let's see about Horace."

She led John and Sebastian back to Horace's office. They found Horace on his knees, crawling around on the floor and patting the carpet.

"Are you looking for this?" Jessica asked, holding out the key.

His face paled. "Oh, dear," he said. "Then you know about the other ledger with the extra angels. Jessica, I'm sorry. It was all so terribly easy to do. If only you had given up more easily, nobody would have been hurt."

"What are you talking about? Wait a minute. Extra angels? Other ledger?"

John pulled out his badge. "Detective John Quincy Jones on special assignment," he said. "I think we're getting a confession here, Ms. Mitchner." He turned to Horace. "Would you care to open up your desk, Mr. Roland? I can get a warrant, if necessary."

Horace shrugged. "No need. I'll give it to you. You might as well know it all." He sighed. "I guess I'm just not cut out to be a crook, anyway. And I would have felt terrible if Chummy had been hurt by that light. I never intended for her to be so near where the light fell. Or the stunt dog. I'm so ashamed! I like dogs, really I do."

He snuffled. "By tomorrow I'd have been on a plane to Brazil, where you couldn't have touched me, and I'd have been eight million dollars' rich. It almost worked. All my life I've been around so much money, and none of it's ever been mine. I just wanted it to be mine. It would have been, too."

"Except for my dog, Sebastian," John said. "If he hadn't been naughty and accidentally taken your key, you might have gotten away with this."

Naughty? Accidentally? Oh, how *could* John! The patch, maybe. But not the key! When would John ever give him credit?

John called the uniformed officers to take Horace in. "I don't think you'll have any more trouble with accidents," he told Jessica. "Horace thought he could close you down and would never have to reveal the names of the angels," he explained. "If four of them had gotten into the gossip columns, the other four would have caught on."

Jessica shook John's hand. "I guess this means that Sebastian won't finish up the picture," she said. "There's only one stunt left—swimming the rain-swollen river while pushing a litter of puppies in a basket."

"Sorry. I've done my job," John said. "It's time to go home."

He'd done his job? John? Humans! Wouldn't the hairy hawkshaw ever get credit? At least they were going home—away from Hollywood and its crazy stunts.

After a sloppy farewell from Chummy and thanks from Rod (at least somebody appreciated his work), Sebastian was grateful to get back to the jet the next day and wing homeward. It seemed impossible that the case had been solved in a twenty-four-hour period and they were back under Chief's impatient eye again.

Sebastian was glad that John had begged a day off—that is, until he found out why. His sneaky human pulled the car up in front of Dear Doggie Obedience School. John was really going to do it to him!

Mumbling under his breath, he trotted alongside John into the registrar's office.

Sebastian was careful to stay at John's side. And when Mrs. Dingle, the instructor, walked over, Sebastian sat and offered his paw politely.

"Ummm," she said. "Lie."

Immediately Sebastian slid to the proper position, toes pointed out, chin horizontal to the floor, eyes on Mrs. Dingle.

She nodded. She threw a rubber ball. "Fetch," she said.

Sebastian dashed to retrieve the ball, then sat in front of Mrs. Dingle, dropping it into her hand.

She lifted one eyebrow questioningly at John. He shrugged apologetically. "He—he doesn't usually— That is, he almost never does that for me."

"Heel," she commanded. "Walkies!"

Sebastian fell into step at her left side and walked when she walked and stopped when she stopped. A West Point cadet couldn't have moved with greater precision. He'd show them!

Mrs. Dingle reached down and patted Sebastian. "Good dog!" she said. She turned to John. "Mr. Jones, frankly, there is nothing wrong with this animal. He is a perfect gentleman. Shame on you, talking about him as if he were naughty! He doesn't need obedience school. Shame, Mr. Jones. Of course, the trouble could be with you. Perhaps you are not setting a good example for this dear doggie. Now, if you'd like to enroll yourself—"

John blushed and sputtered a hasty apology. "Er, ah, that is, no. That is, thank you. Heel!" he commanded.

Sebastian trotted out to the car next to John, a panting grin spread across his face. His human was no match for Sebastian (Super Sleuth). But, then, who was?

About the Author
and Illustrator

MARY BLOUNT CHRISTIAN attended the University of Houston, where she majored in journalism. A veteran author of books for children, she still likes to refer to herself as a "writer." Her titles include ten other Sebastian (Super Sleuth) mysteries, four Ready-to-Read books, and her novel *Growin' Pains*. Ms. Christian lives in Houston, Texas, with her husband, George.

LISA MCCUE is the talented illustrator of the Sebastian series. She lives in Tappan, New York.